SQUIRREL
— IN THE —
HOUSE

by **Vivian Vande Velde**

illustrated by
Steve Björkman

Holiday House / New York

Text copyright © 2016 by Vivian Vande Velde
Illustrations copyright © 2016 by Steve Björkman
All Rights Reserved
HOLIDAY HOUSE is registered in the U.S. Patent and Trademark Office.
Printed and bound in March 2017 at Berryville Graphics, Berryville, VA, USA.

3 5 7 9 10 8 6 4 2
www.holidayhouse.com

Library of Congress Cataloging-in-Publication data
Names: Vande Velde, Vivian, author. | Björkman, Steve, illustrator.
Title: Squirrel in the house / by Vivian Vande Velde ; illustrated by Steve Björkman.
Description: First Edition. | New York : Holiday House, [2016] | Summary: "A
Squirrel narrates this story of a family get-together turned upside down when he
climbs down the chimney to join the festivities"— Provided by publisher.
Identifiers: LCCN 2015035413 | ISBN 9780823436330 (hardcover)
Subjects: | CYAC: Squirrels—Fiction. | Humorous stories.
Classification: LCC PZ7.V3986 Sq 2016 | DDC [Fic]—dc23 LC record available at
http://lccn.loc.gov/2015035413
ISBN 978-0-8234-3877-8 (paperback)

*Dedicated with appreciation to Steve Björkman,
whose lively illustrations brought Twitch to life
in 8 Class Pets—and who encouraged me
to write another story about him*

Contents

Twitch,
the School-yard Squirrel

The dog who lives next door to the yard where I live tells me that people call dogs "man's best friend."

Well, actually, the dog doesn't so much tell me this as he yells it. Usually while he's chasing me. Often the dog gets so angry when he sees me that he tries to catch me. I don't know why he gets angry. I guess some dogs are just highly excitable that way. But when he runs after me, he can only go so far. Then his leash stops him.

I try to point things out to the dog, purely for

educational purposes. I live in the school yard, so I am a very well-educated squirrel. I say, "Man's best friend, huh? You're tied to a tree. You did notice that, didn't you? My friends don't tie me to trees."

Time and again the dog gets so angry about the life lesson I've tried to give that he forgets about his leash. He lunges, he runs out of leash, he bounces back.

Very calmly, not to tease him but only to explain the way things are, I say to the dog, "I think it's squirrels who are man's best friend. That's why the man who lives here ties you up—so you can't bother me."

The dog is not very smart. He does not appreciate my trying to educate him. Sometimes the dog gets so angry he forgets words. He barks the bark that is just noise: "Bark! Bark! Bark!"

I never forget words, and I never bark.

Still, the man who is not the dog's best friend is not very smart, either. He doesn't realize that he doesn't have to tie up the dog to keep him from catching me. I can always climb a tree to get out of the dog's reach.

From the tree, I can drop walnuts onto the dog's head.

Purely for educational purposes, of course.

Inside vs. Outside

Another way that squirrels have a better life than dogs do—besides the whole tied-to-a-tree-with-a-leash thing—is that dogs sometimes have to go Inside with the people. Squirrels never have to go Inside.

Well, we get to go inside trees where there's a hollow, but that's only if we want to. And that's not the same thing anyway.

Inside for dogs means even more rules than dogs have when they're outside. Inside means no running around as fast as you want to, no digging, only eat when the people decide you're hungry and wait for the people to tell you that you need to poop or pee. I know all this because I sometimes hear the man who lives with the dog explaining the rules. Sometimes he explains them very loudly.

There are no rules for squirrels. Except for the obvious: Don't let the owls catch you.

(Dogs don't have to worry about owls. Dogs think that's because most of them are so much bigger than owls. I think it's more likely that dogs don't taste good, and that's why owls don't eat them.)

So we squirrels get to run around as much as we want to, which is good, because we usually want to. We can dig wherever we choose, which usually means where we bury our food to hide it for later. We can eat whenever we want, so long as we remember where we've buried our food. And, of course, we can poop and pee as we see fit. The sense of that goes without saying.

The dog who lives next door to my yard (which is bigger than his yard, by the way—not bragging, just saying), the dog tries to convince me he has it better. "It's about to rain, squirrel," he says, sniffing at the sky. "Master will bring me inside, where it's nice and dry, and you'll be all wet."

"I like rain," I tell the dog. "Rain washes me off. You have to have the man wash you off with a hose and that stuff that bubbles and that he says smells like Tropical Sunset for Dogs with Sensitive Skin. I don't know what tropical sunsets are, but I suspect only tropical sunsets are supposed to smell like tropical sunsets."

"IT'S ABOUT TO RAIN, SQUIRREL."

Sometimes the dog will say, "I smell snow coming. Do you like to wash in the snow, squirrel?"

That just goes to show how not-smart the dog is. "You can't wash in snow," I tell him. "Unless it's melted snow. And melted snow is water, not snow. Didn't your mother teach you anything?"

"But snow is cold," the dog tells me. "Too bad for you that you have to be outside in the cold."

"That's why my blanket comes attached," I say, waving my tail in front of his face. But only when he can't get any closer because of the leash. When snow comes, I wrap my tail around me in my cozy nest in the tree hollow. I'm as warm as I need to be.

But I am curious. I can hear some of what goes on Inside through the walls. And I can look Inside through the windows.

But sometimes I wonder what Inside feels like.

Outside

One day the snow comes down very fast and for a long time. The wind blows from exactly the wrong direction: directly into the hole in my tree so that my cozy nest in the hollow is no longer cozy. The wind howls and whistles. The wind batters my cushion of dead leaves so that they crumble into bitty bits that make me sneeze. The wind ruffles the fur of my tail and wiggles its way into my bones.

Because I'm cold, I cannot sleep. Because I cannot sleep, I grow hungry.

The problem is: I've finished the last batch of summer

nuts and berries that I dug up and brought back to my nest. If I want to eat, I have to dig up another of my food hiding places.

The other problem is: I'm such a good hider, sometimes I have trouble finding my hiding places.

And meanwhile the snow is still coming down.

Which am I more? I ask myself: hungry or cold?

I paw through the scraps of this and that in my nest—nutshells, bark, twigs—hoping to find a piece of something tasty that I might have overlooked.

After I pick up what I suspect may be the same walnut shell I've examined three times already, I toss it outside.

The wind blows it back in, and it bounces off my head.

I look out from the hole in my tree.

The snow covers all the branches of all the trees. On the ground, it has piled up higher than I am tall. Sometimes, when snow is crisp, I can walk on it. Other times, when snow is fluffy, I sink down into it. Whichever kind of snow this is, my paws are going to get cold.

Then I notice the house where the dog lives. I remember the dog saying, "Too bad for you that you have to be outside in the cold."

I realize the dog was inviting me in. That's because everybody loves squirrels. Even the dog. He just sometimes gets excitable.

I have to remember my manners. I will invite the dog to come visit me.

Not that he can climb my tree. Or squeeze through the hole. Or fit in my nest.

But it will still be polite to ask.

After I've visited him.

The house has three doors. Two of them are at ground level and are people-sized, but the third is obviously meant for squirrels. It is squirrel-sized,  and it is on the roof with easy access via tree. The squirrel door is actually the finest of the three, as it has a grand brick entryway. This entryway goes straight down from the roof right into the heart of the house. Sometimes smoke and heat come out of this roofy doorway, but on this day the man who lives with the dog has not turned on the smoke and heat. As though the dog's words weren't enough, this is a clear signal that the man, also, wants me to come in.

People LOVE squirrels. They put feeders out, just for us, high up off the ground so the dogs can't reach them. Sometimes birds eat our food, but we squirrels know it's been put out for us, not them, because of the playgrounds so many people build around our feeders, with rides for sliding and swinging and spinning on. The birds don't use the rides; they only eat the food.

And now both man and dog have invited me in. I can't wait to see what wonders they have prepared for me Inside.

Running fast so that my toes don't get cold, I leap from branch to branch until I'm above the roof. I jump, but my toes must be colder than I thought, and I don't go as far onto the roof as I expected, and the roof is icy, so I slip down toward the edge.

My paws scrabble for something so I won't fall off,

and I catch hold of the metal squirrel ride thingy that most people have all around the edge of their roofs. On rainy days, these things fill with water for slipping and sliding around in, and at the corners of the house, they form slides down to the ground. It's a lot of fun to go down these water slides. The people should build some for themselves. On this cold day the squirrel ride thingy is filled with snow, not water. Still, it's good for catching hold of.

With a squeal, the whole thing pulls away from the roof. The man really should have built it better: I could have gotten hurt! But all is fine. I'm able to scramble back onto the roof and up the outside of the brick entryway to the squirrel door. I sit on the edge and look down. I'm far up, but I can see Inside.

Inside

The brick entry hall that leads down from the squirrel door on the roof is very long. It is also very dark. Not to mention steep. Some of the bricks are slippery because of the soot and ash from when the man makes fire. But I'm very sure-footed.

Until all that soot and ash makes me sneeze.

Then I go down the last bit quite quickly. Not falling. But quickly.

I land on pieces of a cut-apart tree at the bottom. Obviously this is the man's attempt to re-create my tree that is Outside here Inside. It is his way of saying, "Welcome, Twitch."

For a few moments I can't see because of the big black cloud of soot and ash that has come down with me. "Hello," I call out to let everyone know I have arrived, even though I can tell, by listening and smelling, that neither the dog nor the man is in this room. That's okay. I can make myself at home, which is what good hosts, if they were here, would tell me to do.

Once the black cloud settles, I see that the floor beyond it is white and it looks fluffy, sort of like snow, but not cold. This is convenient for not getting lost because I'm leaving little black footprints wherever I set my paws down.

From another part of Inside, I hear the dog. "Bark. Bark. Bark," he says, too excited to form words. I hear the nails on his not-good-for-climbing doggy paws as he comes running on a hard surface toward the part of Inside where I am. I hear the man yelling, "Cuddles!

Cuddles!" which is what he
calls the dog. The dog calls
himself Wolf-Born, the Swift
and Ferocious. I call the dog
the dog.

The dog runs into the room where
I am and immediately sees me. He
looks so excited, I decide we need
some distance between us.

I jump off the fluffy white
surface that isn't snow, back on top
of the pile of wood. "Hey, dog," I say.

He says, "You don't belong inside. Out! Out! Out!
Out! Out!"

I say, "I just got here. Thanks for inviting me, by
the way."

He repeats, "Out! Out! Out! Out! Out!"

I scramble up the outside of the brick entryway that
I used the inside of to come down from the roof. There's
a ledge here, where the man who lives with the dog
has gathered things. Squirrels mostly gather nuts and
berries and seeds. People gather all sorts of things that
even people must know are not things to eat. I don't
recognize what the things are that the man has gathered
except for some pinecones dusted with something that

makes them sparkle and a container with water and flowers (even though there are no flowers Outside, on account of the snow).

I'm so quick that the dog—I might have mentioned he's not very bright—hasn't seen where I've gone. So he starts looking for me by pawing through the pieces of tree where I landed when I first came in. The pieces of tree tumble out of their neat little pile and roll onto the white not-snow floor. The dog keeps barking, now asking, "Where are you? Where'd you go?"

Which sounds to me like we're playing hide-and-seek. So I step behind one of the I-don't-know-what-it-is things on the ledge and say, "Here."

The dog looks up but can't see me. He goes back to digging at the pile of wood.

I step behind another I-don't-know-what-it-is thing. I say, "Here."

The dog sniffs at the air. "Where?" he demands.

I think he's asking for too many hints, but I can see he really isn't very good at this game. I go to step behind the flowers, to announce, "Here," once more, but the container isn't as steady as it should be, and the whole thing—container, flowers, and water—falls off the ledge and lands on the floor with a crash.

The dog tries to leap up onto the ledge with me, but he's not a good climber.

I encourage him, saying, "Here! Here! Here!" as I dodge from behind thing to thing to thing on the ledge.

"Not the lamp!" the dog shouts as a tall glass thing that is like the sun, but smaller, teeters.

Okay, so I move.

"Not the picture of Master's mother!" the dog complains. Pictures look like the things they look like, except flat.

I recognize Master's mother as the woman who lives in this house with the man and the dog.

Okay, so I move again.

"Not Master's first-prize trophy for being voted the best principal in the state!" the dog howls. He's pacing back and forth on the floor below the ledge as though he's trying to decide what to do.

Then he decides.

The dog jumps onto a chair and from there to the low table that has another sun-like lamp, and from there onto the ledge.

"Good jump!" I cheer. It's polite to acknowledge someone's improved effort. I leap onto the cloth that is hanging over the window and climb to the branch-like metal thing on top. "Now I'm here!"

Which is when the man who lives here with his mother comes running into the room.

"Hello, man," I call out, even though I know people aren't as smart as animals and can't understand us. "Thank you for inviting me." But the dog is making too much noise for the man to hear me.

In another moment, the man is making too much noise, too. "Cuddles!" he yells. "What are you doing? Come down immediately!"

He grabs hold of the dog's collar, but by this time the

dog realizes how high up he is, and he freezes in fear.

The man has to put his arms around the dog and lift him down. While he's doing this, the man's elbow knocks into the lamp, and the lamp falls. Clearly the man has a love for leashes. Not only does he often tie the dog to the tree in the yard, but in here there's a leash that fastens the lamp to the wall. So it's the man's own fault when this leash pulls taut and topples most of the pictures, including Mother's.

People run into the room. Apparently the man has invited quite a few guests in out of the cold. Which is fine. As guest of honor, I'm happy to meet them.

The man's mother starts yelling. "Sonny!" she demands. "Why are you trying to put that fool dog of yours up on my mantel?"

"I'm not," the man says, just as his foot comes down on the spilled water from the container of flowers. Still holding the dog, the man slides into the low table and knocks over that lamp, too.

Inside is more exciting than I thought it would be.

The mother starts yelling at the man; the man is yelling at the dog; the dog is barking his beside-himself no-words bark; and the other guests are all giving advice that sounds pretty useless to me.

Things like:

"Hold that dog." (The man already is.)

And, "Somebody should get a mop." (Nobody does.)

And, "That rug will never come clean." (Maybe they could use Tropical Sunset for Dogs with Sensitive Skin to wash it.)

Anyway, nobody notices me, sitting on top of the window.

"Gramma! Gramma!" the two little boys in this crowd of adult people yell. "What's Uncle Buzz doing?"

"I haven't a clue," the mother says, shaking her head. To the man she says, "You put that fool dog Outside before he breaks any more of my things."

The man is sitting sprawled out on the chair, the yapping dog on his lap. The dog has left black paw prints on the ledge, on the table, on the chair, and on the man. The man says, "It's too cold for Cuddles to stay Outside."

"Well, then, lock him in the basement." Mother stomps her feet as she leaves the room.

"Wow!" exclaims the smaller child. "This is more fun than we ever have at home."

I know exactly how he feels.

People Children

The dog is barking out: "That worthless rodent is on the curtain rod!" But the man can't understand the dog any more than the man can understand me.

"Cuddles!" the man shouts. "Stop that howling!"

The man has hold of the dog's collar and is dragging him out of the room. The other guests follow, still trailing advice:

"You need to give that dog a stern talking-to."

"You need to send that dog to obedience school."

"You need to replace that dog with a cat."

"Hey!" I call from where I'm sitting, on what the dog called the curtain rod. "Where's everyone going? Wait for me."

If the branch-like metal thing where I'm sitting is the curtain rod, then the cloth must be the curtain. I've just learned something new. Not necessarily something useful, but something new. I climb down the curtain, but I'm delayed because one of my nails gets caught in the cloth. It takes quite a bit of tugging and a little bit of biting before I get free. Now the curtain has holes in it. This is a good thing, because before, the curtain blocked the view to Outside, but now everybody will be able to see Outside without having to push the curtain out of their way. I have helped the people, but there's no one left to see my improvement. At this point, I'm the only one in the room.

I start to follow the people. As guest of honor, it's my duty not to ignore them—but on my way out I notice another little table. Sitting on this one is a bowl of nuts. Nuts are the best thing ever. And guess what—they're already out of their shells! How thoughtful of the dog and his people! I change my mind: My first duty is not to find the other guests but to show my appreciation to my hosts.

After I've eaten enough that I feel full for now, I look around to see where I can bury the rest of the nuts for later. There are two containers that hold dirt and plants. In one of the containers is a little tree, but not like the ones I'm used to outside. It only has a few branches, and it's much scrawnier. I try climbing it, because that's what squirrels do. But I could never rest in its branches: The whole thing bends under my weight. The people didn't think this out very well. Still, I'm able to bury several of the nuts in the dirt beneath the tree.

The second container is smaller. Its plant has flowers, but it isn't very hardy: Several of the blooms fall off the plant while I'm digging beneath it. They aren't even good-tasting flowers. I wonder what the dog and the man and the man's mother were thinking when they decided to grow this plant. Its container is only good for holding a couple of nuts.

I hide the rest here and there about the room: under the cushions of the chairs, behind the curtains, and in the shoes that the guests have left by the front door. I don't know why people wear shoes, or why these people have taken theirs off. Some of the shoes smell worse than the dog.

It's while I'm burying the last of the nuts in the last of the shoes that I hear a soft voice say, "Hey! Hello, squirrel."

It's the smaller of the two people children. He's so small that I think he's probably too young to go to school. This might be a problem.

Living in a school yard, I know all about school. School starts at that time of year when the very first leaves are just beginning to change color and when, if the air hasn't already gotten nippy at night, it will soon. Of course everybody loves squirrels, but the ones who love squirrels best are those children who are just old enough to go to school. And during those first few days of school, the year's new batch of children-just-old-enough-to-go-to-school always want to catch us and bring us home with them. The little boys chase us, but the girls are worse. They say, "Oooo, that squirrel would look so cute in my doll's pink sparkly dress." I have very nice fur. I don't need a pink sparkly dress.

The teachers at the school have to teach the new batch of children the same thing they had to teach last year's batch: None of us who live in the yard—not squirrels, or chipmunks, or rabbits, or mice, or voles, or robins, or the butterflies who are passing through, or worms or even the beetles—not one of us wants to go home with the children.

So I'm looking at the boy—this other guest in the

house of the man and the woman and the dog—and I'm thinking: I don't believe this one knows that whole please-don't-try-to-catch-the-squirrel thing.

I especially think this when he extends his hand toward me and comes closer.

From the direction where all the people went when they left, I hear another voice, the older, slightly bigger boy calling him, telling him it's time to eat.

I take a moment to ask myself if I'm ready to eat again.

Meanwhile, the smaller boy turns to answer, and I use the opportunity to jump back to the pile of wood where I first landed when I came Inside, and I snuggle down low.

When he looks again, the younger boy no longer sees me. "Hey!" he says. "Where did you go?" And he steps to where he last saw me, by the shoes near the door.

The larger boy enters the room. Sounding impatient, he tells the smaller one, "Gramma said now."

The smaller one picks up the shoe by which he saw me standing. He turns the shoe upside down and three almonds and a pecan fall out.

Next starts an argument between the two boys, with the older pointing out why it is not acceptable behavior to store foodstuffs in people's shoes.

The smaller one denies putting the nuts there and says, "The squirrel did it."

Of course the larger boy hasn't seen me. He points out why it is not acceptable behavior to make up stories.

When the smaller one denies that he is making up stories, the older boy points out why it is not acceptable behavior to delay long enough that one of the parents will come looking for them.

The older boy encourages the younger to get moving by pulling him toward the door.

The younger boy tries to resist, but the bigger boy is big enough that the smaller one is sliding in the direction the bigger one wants him to go in.

At which point, the smaller one grabs hold of that scrawny not-good-for-climbing tree to keep from being dragged away.

The older keeps pulling, the younger keeps sliding . . . and the tree tips over, knocking down another of those lamp-things, which hits the floor with a crash.

Wow! People sure keep a lot of breakable things Inside!

The other guests come running in, and—once again—everyone talks really loudly and without listening to anybody else. Mostly, they talk about why it is not acceptable behavior to not mind, and to break things.

I appreciate having been invited Inside to get warm and to eat nuts, but how's a poor squirrel to get an after-eating nap with all this noise? So I climb back up the entryway, cross the roof, jump onto the branch of my sturdy, climbable tree, and go back into my nice nest hollow. It's cold here, but it's quiet. And my tummy is full, which is always a good thing.

I'm just about to fall asleep when I happen to glance once more out of the hole and in the direction of the house where the dog and the man and the man's mother live, and where their guests have gathered.

The smaller boy has just come out of the front door.

Mostly people children who are that small do not travel alone, so I keep one eye open to see if anybody is following him.

Nobody.

By the way he's stomping his feet, I can tell he's angry. Probably because of the whole not-breaking-things conversation.

He is wearing his shoes. I'm guessing he took the nuts out first, unless he's keeping them there to eat later. But the only body covering he has is what he was wearing Inside.

People aren't lucky enough to have fur, much less an attached-blanket tail. Mostly people children wear a lot of body covering when they go Outside. Especially in the snow.

This, I think, is not good.

Not a Good Idea

A polite guest of honor is alert to be sure the other guests don't feel overlooked. Therefore, one of my duties as guest of honor at the dog's house is to see that everyone is comfortable. I do not believe the smaller boy could be comfortable when he is Outside with body covering that is meant for Inside.

I get out of my nest, which at this moment I am positive must be the warmest, coziest, most comfortable nest in the best tree hollow in the world. As soon as I step through the hole in my tree, both my eyes snap open wide at the cold.

I find a branch that overhangs the front section of the yard, and I run along its length, chattering at the boy: "Hey! Hey! Hey!" It would be too much to expect the boy to understand, but I'm hoping to at least catch his attention.

Either he does not hear me or he's ignoring me.

And, of course, there's no reason for him to ignore me.

I jump one tree over, where there are lower-hanging branches. "Hey! Hey! Hey!"

Nope.

I leap onto the clothesline and use that to get to the last tree I can reach without going to ground level and putting my little paws onto that cold, cold snow.

He has his head down as he walks into the wind. His arms are wrapped around himself, and his shoulders are up, which is not much protection against the snow

that is falling. He has to step high to make his way through the snow that is on the ground. I suspect that he's already regretting his decision to come outside but is too stubborn to go back.

"Hey!" I call.

I sigh and climb down the tree.

Oooo, that snow is cold!

I jump from foot to foot to foot to foot, but that snow is not going to get less cold anytime soon.

The boy is not heading toward the back of the house and to the school yard—which would be the one place that would make a little sense, if he wanted to play there the same way I like to play on the rides around the squirrel feeders. Instead, he walks on the sidewalk in front of the house—or, rather, where the sidewalk would be if it wasn't for the snow. My guess is that he isn't so much walking *to* someplace as away.

The snow is fluffy, not good for walking on top of, so I follow where the boy has walked, bounding from footprint to footprint.

"Hey!" I call again.

This time he hears me and he turns around.

I have to call, "Hey!" again before he figures out to look down.

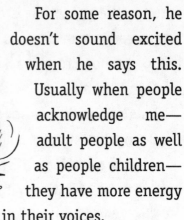

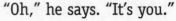

"Oh," he says. "It's you."

For some reason, he doesn't sound excited when he says this. Usually when people acknowledge me— adult people as well as people children— they have more energy in their voices.

I figure maybe he's too cold to be enthusiastic.

But then he turns back the way he was going and continues walking.

"Hey! Hey! Hey!" I say again.

He keeps walking.

I keep chattering, "Hey!"

Finally he gets to the corner, where a street cuts across his way. Now he stops. He considers. He sighs.

Because I am a school-yard squirrel and very well educated, I know what's going on. Small people children are not allowed to cross streets without adult people supervision.

I tell him, "Now might be a good time to turn back." I'm guessing it probably sounds to him pretty much the same as when I told him, "Hey! Hey! Hey!"

Once more he faces me. "Haven't you gotten me into enough trouble?" he asks.

Me? It wasn't my fault the other guests all turned on him.

But still, I feel sorry for him.

Even if he doesn't have the sense to come in out of the cold.

Young squirrels are better trained than that. They would know to take cover in the cold.

But at least the boy is trained well enough that he doesn't cross the street. He turns the corner and keeps walking. And walking and walking and walking.

Until he gets to the next corner.

It must suddenly occur to him that if he turns enough corners, he will be right back where he started.

"It's too wintry a day to run away from home," I advise him. "This is not a good idea. You can try again in the spring."

I don't know if he understands this or if he's simply come to the same thought at the same time. His shoulders slump, a sign that he has given up. He turns around to face the direction from which he has just come.

I chatter encouragement.

He takes a step. And his feet slide out from under him. He lands flat on his back, one leg bent under him, the wind knocked out of him.

I chatter more encouragement.

The boy tries to stand, but the leg that was bent under him buckles, so that he falls back into the snow. He tries again. But the leg can't support him. Now that he wants to go home, he cannot.

Lying in the snow, unable to get up, he starts crying. Squirrels don't cry, but people do. I don't know enough about crying to be able to tell if this is mad crying, or sad crying, or scared crying, or cold crying, or hurt crying.

Surely the adult people will come and fetch him, I think. People parents will be as frantic as squirrel parents would be over a lost child.

Except that the wind and the snow are quickly covering the footprints leading here.

How will they ever find him?

Table Manners

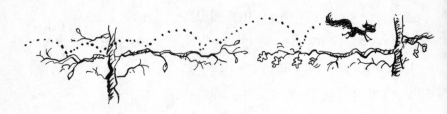

The snow covering the sidewalk is too high to let me walk easily. And besides, sidewalks are not the squirrel way of doing things. Traveling by tree is a lot easier. And a lot more fun.

Elm to maple to spruce . . .

I do get somewhat distracted when I come across a woodpecker huddled in his tree hollow. True, I accidentally stepped on his tail. But that's no reason for him to say, "Hey, watch it, fur-for-brains!"

I tell him, "Just because you have a headache from

banging your head against tree trunks to get at bugs is no reason to get annoyed with me. Try eating something easier to get to, and see if you're less cranky."

Still, I'm on a mission, so I can't visit long.

Two walnut trees, a crab apple, then up into my own maple tree, with that wonderfully warm, cozy nest, which is going to be so incredibly comfortable to snuggle down into . . .

I catch sight of the house where the dog lives and remember the other guest, the little boy, hurt and out in the cold. Without a cozy nest. I sigh.

Then I again jump onto the roof of the house and make my way to and then down that long entryway, landing once more on the pieces of wood that are at the bottom.

The people are gone from the room, but someone has picked up both the lamp-thing and the scrawny tree that

knocked it down. Each appears to have pieces missing.

Beyond this room, I see a long, skinny room with many doors and also stairs. I know about stairs. The school has three stairs going up to the entrance. Here, there are a lot more than three. Even though I am a well-educated squirrel, my brain gets to feeling numb with numbers bigger than three. I stand at the bottom and count, "One, two, three—one time. One, two, three—two times. One, two, three—three times." There are still more stairs. Obviously more stairs than it's worth counting. So I don't climb them.

I notice voices coming through one doorway, but interesting smells coming from another doorway.

I go to the interesting-smells doorway. This room has big metal things, one with knobs and handles and a dark window; the other almost reaches the ceiling and hums. They are not as big as the cars and buses that bring the people children to school, but just as mysterious.

There is also a long counter with various containers on it. Finally, something about the people who live here makes sense!—because these containers contain food, which is what containers should contain. I get up on the counter to investigate.

One container is short and squat—like the dog's water bowl that he has Outside in warm weather. This bowl has something that's red and smells like strawberries, but it doesn't look like strawberries because it's one big, almost see-through piece. It jiggles when I poke at it. I

scoop out a pawful. Its taste isn't exactly strawberries, but it puts me in mind of strawberries, which doesn't usually happen when the snow is falling, so I decide I like it after all.

Another of these bowls contains potato chips. I know potato chips from the school yard. They are the best thing ever. I eat two or three of those. Maybe four.

The trouble with potato chips is that they make you thirsty, so I spit the last piece back out into the bowl for someone else to enjoy.

Looking around to see if there is a bowl of water, I bump into a tall, skinny container. It falls over, and what's inside spills outside and drips off the edge of the counter onto the floor. What spills looks like water, except it has bubbles. It tastes sweeter than regular water and is sticky, and it makes my nose feel fizzy. I sneeze into the container of cupcakes. I know cupcakes from school celebrations.

The last bowl has sunflower seeds. I love sunflower seeds. They are the best thing ever. Even though I already ate until I was full, time has passed, so I eat the seeds.

By now, I've worked off the chill I got trekking through the snow Outside, and I'm just thinking about taking a nap when I remember why I came Inside:

because of the small boy who has wandered off. And his frantic parents.

Not that they actually seem frantic. They aren't even looking for him.

Well, then, I'll look for them.

I follow my ears to the doorway, through which I can still hear people-talk.

This room has a long table, and the other guests are sitting around it. "One, two, three—one time," I count. But then I decide it doesn't make any difference how many other guests there are. More than three. Fewer than during recess at school.

I stand in the doorway and call out: "Have any of you lost a smallish people child?"

The people keep talking to each other and don't notice me.

The trouble is they're noisy, which I can't do anything about, plus I'm on the short side. Below their eye level. People have a tendency not to look up or down but only straight ahead. That I know how to fix.

There is a cloth, very similar to the curtain in the other room, but this one covers the table. The larger boy is sitting next to an empty space, which might be where the smaller boy is supposed to sit. I jump and catch hold of the cloth. Everything on the table shifts a bit in my direction.

The people all slam their hands down onto the table covering to keep it from moving, then turn to the boy and start telling him to behave.

He protests that he hasn't done anything, but then he looks down and sees me hanging on to the cloth next to his leg. He jumps up so quickly that his chair falls over.

This gives me even more space, so I continue climbing up the cloth until I'm on top of the table. There's lots more food here, which is tempting to a squirrel who hasn't eaten in . . .

Oh, wait. I guess I've just eaten. But it's still tempting. Even so, I tell myself now is not the time to get distracted—I'm on a mission. And I no longer need to worry about the noise level because no one is talking anymore—they're all staring at me. Well, that's convenient. I say, "Which one of you belongs to the smaller boy?"

One of the people screams, which is just plain rude, no matter how you look at it.

The man who lives here with the dog jumps to his feet, and he grabs one of the bowls off the table. He flips it upside down, which sends pieces of lettuce and cucumbers and tomatoes and radish bits showering down on me. Then he tries to put the bowl over my head, but

I zigzag and avoid him. Either he wants to make sure I don't leave until I've eaten, or it's that whole catch-a-squirrel-and-bring-him-home thing.

Except that I already am in his home.

People get confused so easily.

Anyway, I don't have time for this. I run and bound down the length of the table, only occasionally landing in someone's food, then leap onto the curtain—the real curtain, the one covering the window—and climb up onto the curtain rod. There, I take a moment to lick off the food that's gotten between my toes. Yummy! I don't know where people gather their food, but it tends to be tasty.

Meanwhile, the man has moved his chair against the wall near me, and he's climbed onto it, so I jump onto a tall piece of furniture that's made of wood and glass and that holds bowls and other people stuff. The whole thing wobbles, and the mother who lives here with the man and the dog really starts screaming now, no doubt worried that I might get hurt. But I'm sure-footed and make it safely across the top of that furniture till I can drop back onto the table at the end that's closest to the door. The cloth skids along under me, carrying me and the food and bowls with it, but I jump a heartbeat before the whole thing slithers off the table onto the floor behind me. Several of the bowls bounce on the floor. Several definitely do not bounce. I run out of that room, through the long, skinny room, and back into the room where I originally started.

I sit and wait for someone to follow, so I can lead them outside.

Amazingly, no one takes the hint. Instead, I hear them—still in the room where they were eating— yelling such things as, "Oh my!" and "What was that?"

What was that? Really? Like they've never seen a squirrel before?

Then finally—finally!—someone points out that the smaller child was obviously telling the truth about a squirrel being in the house. And that it must have been the squirrel who caused all the damage in the other room.

Excuse me? That was the dog. And the man. And the two people children.

But in any case, they say the child has sulked upstairs long enough after being scolded for something he didn't do, and someone needs to fetch him—while someone else needs to call Pest Control.

I think it's pretty mean of them to call the boy a pest in need of control, but sometimes families can be like that.

Someone goes up the stairs to fetch him, and that's when the fuss really begins—when they can't find him.

They look upstairs and down. Two of them even walk right by me and open the front door, never noticing me standing right there, chattering, "I know! I know! I know where he is!"

The snow is still falling, falling, falling. The people say, "He wouldn't have gone out in that," and they close the door again.

These people are hopeless!

Hello, Dog?

How can I get through to these people that their second-smallest guest is outside and needs help?

I could jump on one of them, I think, but there's always the possibility that if I do, that person will hold on to me, and eventually I'll end up in a pink sparkly dress. I'm not willing to risk that. Girls can't be trusted. Even girls who look like adults.

I run back and forth in front of them, but not close enough for anyone to catch me. The trouble is that at this point they have gotten more concerned to find the missing child than they are to catch me.

Why can't they understand me?

Then it comes to me: I am a highly educated squirrel. These people aren't smart enough to follow what I am trying to tell them.

What I need to do is find someone who is in between squirrel-smart and people-smart.

And then that answer comes to me, too: the dog!

The man said he was going to put the dog in the basement. I don't know what "in the basement" means. Is in the basement like in one of the containers for holding food? I run back into the room where there was the food and those big metal things, including—I suddenly remember—the one with the window.

But the window is dark, and I can't see anything even when I hang upside down from the handle. I tap against the glass. "You in there, dog?" I ask.

No answer.

No smell of him, either.

No, wait—there is. I sniff with my highly developed squirrel nose. There is a faint scent of the dog nearby.

I follow my nose to another door. "Hello, dog?" I call. "Are you in the basement on the other side of this door?"

There is a loud thump as the dog throws himself against the door. "Squirrel!" he barks. "Wait until I get my paws on you!" The door rattles in its frame as the dog hurls himself at it again. And again. And again.

It's a challenge to work with someone who is so excitable. "Stop barking," I tell him. "I need you to do something for me."

"You," the dog says in a sputtering kind of bark, "you need me to do something for you?"

I'm relieved that the dog isn't as not-smart as I worried, that he can—in fact—grasp the situation.

"Yes," I say.

"Oh, well, then," the dog says. "Sure."

I scratch my ear, trying to catch hold of a thought that flitters around in my brain. But it moves too quickly and is gone. "Okay," I say. "Well, the first thing you have to do is, you have to come out from in the basement."

The dog's voice is a bit strained— I'm guessing because he's so eager to help me—as he says, "Squirrel. The. Door. Is. Shut."

"Yes, it is," I agree. "Open it."

The dog bounces against the door once more. "IT DOESN'T OPEN!"

Being a highly educated squirrel, I see the problem. "Back away," I tell the dog. "There's a hook latch." I know about hook latches because some people use them on the sheds where they store their squirrel food—in order to keep out the neighborhood cats. I climb onto the counter, then jump at the door latch. The hook pops up and the door opens. I say, "Ta-dah! Now you can help me."

But that same thought that flittered before is hovering again, and there's something about the look in the dog's eyes as he stands there face-to-face with me ... And I realize I never told him what I needed his help for, so—considering that—he agreed to help awfully quickly.

It suddenly occurs to me that I might want to a little bit of distance between me and the dog before I take the time to explain about the smaller boy.

The dog and I jump at the same time: He jumps at me, and I jump straight up.

I twist midair—squirrels are very fit and flexible, and we make excellent natural acrobats. So I go up, sideways, and down. The down is into . . . I don't know what to call it: a container or a piece of furniture. It's taller than the dog, but not quite half as tall as people. Inside is hollow and there are empty wrapper papers and eggshells and coffee grounds and a wad of used gum and some toast crusts—with peanut butter on them! I love peanut butter! It's the best thing ever.

But before I can cram more than one crust inside my cheek, the dog runs at the container/furniture and knocks it over. Everything spills out—including me.

I race across the slippery floor, my feet going faster than the rest of me does. My plan is to go through the long room with the stairs and all the other doorways and to go through the doorway that leads to the room where I came in. I will go up the curtain and talk to the dog from there. I don't think he has the proper attitude to listen while he's chasing me. He's doing that no-words bark and I doubt my words would sink in.

But a bunch of the other guests are standing in the doorway's room. One of them is crying about the lost smaller boy, and the others are trying to comfort her—and there are just too many feet in my way.

I skid around a turn and change direction: I go up the stairs.

No Pets in Mother's Room!

I know that the dog can't climb trees, and I'm hoping he can't climb stairs, either.

But no, I hear him thudding his way up after me.

I run into the first room I get to. Inside is a long, low, wide piece of furniture where I can see that the guests have laid their Outside clothes, like snakes who have shed their skins. I jump onto that, thinking I can burrow.

But the dog has either seen me or smelled me. He barks, "No pets in Master's mother's room! No pets on Master's mother's bed!"

The dog doesn't listen to his own rule. He jumps up there with me and starts digging through the clothes, trying to find me.

I wiggle out and jump to a higher piece of furniture. This one has a ledge—which I figure the dog can get to—but also a tall mirror attached to the back. A mirror is like a window at night—you can't see through it; it shows what's on this side. There are mirrors at the school in what are called the restrooms. (I haven't a clue about why they're called that, so don't even ask.) Anyway, this mirror has a wooden frame around it, and I can climb that if I need to go higher.

Meanwhile, the dog has still not discovered that I am not underneath the pile of people's Outside clothes, even though he's knocked most of them onto the floor.

We are wasting time.

"Hey, dog!" I call.

But he's too intent on barking and digging through the clothes, and he doesn't hear me.

On the ledge where I'm standing are all sorts of shiny things and containers. One of the containers has powder in it that smells—sort of—like Tropical Sunset for Dogs with Sensitive Skin.

I push the container to the edge of where I'm standing.

I shove.

The container goes flying, a blizzard of powder landing on the floor, on Master's mother's bed, on the Outside clothes and on the dog.

The dog coughs and sneezes and finally—finally!—for a moment isn't barking.

I shout at him, "The smaller boy is outside! He's hurt his leg! He has no Outside clothing on! It's cold and windy and snowy, and the other guests are looking for him, but they don't know where he is!"

The dog bites at an itch. He doesn't agree to help me, but he doesn't start barking again, either.

I say, "The boy is all alone in the snow. The people keep looking Inside, not Out."

The dog looks frustrated. He wants to keep chasing me—he is, after all, a dog—but he asks, "The boy is Outside? Hurt?"

"Outside," I repeat. "Hurt."

My words reach the dog. He tells me, "It's too cold for people to be Outside without their coats and hats and mittens."

I say, "I think that's what I just said."

The dog says, "Someone needs to fetch him."

I say, "That *is* what I just said!" And I jump down to the floor. I will lead the dog out the door, downstairs, Outside, and to the boy.

But suddenly the man who lives here is standing in the door to Mother's room. He says, "What in the world—?" But he must decide he knows the answer to his question after all, because he stops asking and moves to block the whole doorway. He says, "Good work, Cuddles!"

I assume he means about finding me, not about all the clothing on the floor, or the powder on everything. Not to mention the eggshells-and-coffee-grounds trail the dog has left.

The man has a big net, like the children in the school yard sometimes use to try to catch butterflies.

Is there a butterfly in here? Usually they all go away for the winter.

I look around but can't see one.

Then I realize: I am the butterfly.

With the man blocking the way out, I stand on the floor looking up at him. I can't go to the left, and I can't go to the right. It will do no good to go back and climb onto the mirror because the man's net has a long handle.

So I go up.

I launch myself at the man's knee, and then, before he can react, I climb the rest of the way up his leg, over his belly, across his chest, and up to his shoulder. From there, I leap over and behind him.

The man screams. He is just as loud and shrill as the little girls in the school yard, even though I'm already off and running toward the stairs.

"Come on!" I yell to the dog.

The man is still blocking the door. He has dropped the net, though, and he's patting his body as though to make sure I'm not still on him.

The dog runs between the man's legs.

Oh. I guess I could have gone that way, too.

To the Rescue

As the dog runs by me, I jump onto his back and grab hold of his collar. I'm a faster runner than he is, but I'd only have to wait for him to catch up. Besides, riding is more fun.

The dog lets out a high-pitched yip, which I guess means his coat isn't as thick as my claws are long, but he doesn't bark at me to get off.

Together we race down the stairs.

The cluster of guests hears the dog coming, and they get out of our way fast.

"How do we get out?" I ask the dog as we run to the front door. "Can you climb up the squirrel entryway?"

"The what?" the dog asks. "There's no entry for squirrels."

I can tell that he doesn't want to admit there's a door for me but not for him. "The long brick entryway from the roof," I explain.

He shakes his head, which makes me—holding on to his collar—bounce alarmingly.

I say, "That ends in the pile of wood the man built to remind me of the trees Outside? So that I would feel at home? In the room with the floor like snow, except not cold?"

The dog doesn't seem to be catching on at all.

I once more revise my estimate about how not-smart he is. "Where you were digging when you were trying to find me, before the man put you in the basement."

"The chimney?" the dog asks.

Obviously, he's just making up words to hide the fact that there's a squirrel door.

"Yeah, sure," I say. "The chimbly."

"No," the dog says. "I can't climb up there."

I'd been hoping, since he did better with the stairs than I'd have thought.

The dog says, "But I know how to get out."

He sits in front of the door to Outside and howls: "I gotta pee! I gotta pee! I gotta pee! Oh, boy, do I ever gotta pee! Somebody better let me out 'cause I gotta pee now!" He scratches at the door.

I say, "I didn't think people could understand when we talk."

He says, "They can understand this." He increases the whine of his barking. "Oooo, somebody better let me out soon, 'cause I really, really gotta pee!"

The man's mother hurries into the room, grumbling, "Of all the inconvenient times . . ." She calls over her shoulder, "Sonny, I'm letting your fool dog out before he wets on my rug."

We hear the man running down the stairs, having finally gotten over my using him as a jungle gym. He shouts, "Wait!"

But by then the woman has opened the door.

She squints at the dog as he dashes Outside, carrying me with him, and I hear her ask in a scolding tone, "What have you got matted in your fur?" But I don't know if she's seen me, hanging on for dear life, or if she means her powder that he's wearing.

The dog sniffs the snow that covers the boy's footprints on the front walk. "Master's mother's powder is clogging up my nose," he says. "I can't smell anything else."

"To the corner," I direct him, "away from the school."

It's just as bumpy with the dog going over the snowdrifts as it was with him going down the stairs. Not that I would prefer running in the snow myself.

"Around the corner," I say, "to the next corner. I'll tell you when to stop."

But I don't need to. He sees the smaller boy, still sitting huddled on the sidewalk, and the dog puts on a burst of speed that actually shakes me off his back.

I pick myself up and dust the snow off my belly. The dog has run up to the boy and is licking his face. The boy looks half frozen, but happy to see the dog. "Cuddles!" he says, his voice sounding all shivery. He wraps his arms around the dog and buries his face in the dog's fur.

I hear the squeaky crunch! crunch! crunch! of someone who is heavy walking fast on new snow.

It's the man. As soon as he sees the boy, he runs the rest of the way. He's put on his Outside clothing, though he hasn't taken the time to fasten it. Now he hurriedly takes it off and wraps the smaller boy in it. He tells the little boy everything will be all right, and he rubs the boy's hands and blows warm breath on them, and he tells him again everything will be all right, and that everyone was worried, and that everything will be all right, and good thing Cuddles is such a good tracker—he's such a good tracker, he deserves a gold star—and everything will be all right, and it's time to go home now. And that everything will be all right.

He picks the boy up to carry him, and he says, "Come, Cuddles." And then he sees me.

He gives me the same squinty-eyed look his mother gave the dog at the door.

Then he shakes his head and says, "Can't be." Then he asks, "Can it?"

"Certainly," I say. "And thanks for all the food."

As I scamper up a tree, the dog calls after me, "Not badly done. For a rodent."

I pause long enough to call down, "Yeah, and whatever a gold star is, if it's something to eat, I deserve at least half of it!"

And the man starts walking home, once again assuring the previously lost little one that everything will be all right.

Home Sweet Home

I take the shortcut—traveling via tree. But I get sidetracked when I notice a mountain ash tree that still has a few berries. Mountain ash berries are the best thing ever.

So I get back to my tree at the same time that the dog and the man and the smaller child arrive at their home.

Several of the guests have put on their Outside clothes and have come out of the house just in time to greet them. They make such a fuss about how cold the smaller child must be and how lucky he is that he only twisted his ankle and didn't break it that they keep the man from carrying him Inside where it's warmer.

I hear the man tell how Cuddles tracked the boy in the snow and led the way directly to him.

I let the dog get the praise, even though, actually, it was me.

The man's mother gets on her knees, in the snow, in order to hug the dog. She calls him a most excellent hound.

Which I figure has to be a step better than being called a fool dog.

Though, of course, not as good as being called a squirrel.

They all go in the house, and the last thing I hear is Mother calling to everyone to gather around for cupcakes and potato chips to celebrate.

I consider accepting Mother's invitation, which— strictly speaking—would be the polite thing to do. But even though cupcakes are the best thing ever, I decide my stomach really couldn't hold one more bite of food. There's just so much a guest of honor can be expected to do.

So for now I decide not to go back Inside—it's too noisy and complicated in there with all those extra guests visiting, and they aren't all well behaved. How is a hardworking squirrel supposed to get a nap? Instead, I go inside my tree and wrap my tail around myself for warmth and coziness. I close my eyes and start to dream about cupcakes.

I really need to ask the dog, sometime, what kind of tree or bush people gather cupcakes from.

I wonder if it could be that scrawny tree they keep Inside, or the plant with the flowers that didn't taste very good. That would explain a lot.

Come spring blossoming, I'll have to go back Inside to check. Maybe the dog and I can share cupcakes together. After all, I'm highly educated, but he knows his way around a people house—even if he thinks dogs are man's best friend, when we all know squirrels are. Squirrels are everybody's best friend. And, really, sharing cupcakes with a friend is the best thing ever.

Don't miss Squirrel and Cuddles in

8 Class Pets + 1 Squirrel ÷ 1 Dog = Chaos